W9-DEV-719

Barnicle and Husk ™

THE ADVENTURE BEGINS

by Mary Shields

Barnicle & Husk, The Adventure Begins, Published September, 2017

Interior and Cover Illustrations: Bob Ostrom
Cover and Interior Layout Design: Shields Design Studio (SDG Direct, Ltd.)
Editorial and Proofreading: Taylor Morris, Ashley Fedor, Karen Grennan

 SDP Publishing Solutions   Barnicle and Husk

Published by SDP Publishing, an imprint of SDP Publishing Solutions, LLC.
For more information about this book contact Lisa Akoury-Ross at
SDP Publishing by email at info@SDPPublishing.com.

All rights reserved. No part of the material protected by this copyright
notice may be reproduced or utilized in any form or by any means,
electronic or mechanical, including photocopying, recording, or by
any information storage and retrieval system, without written permission
from the copyright owner.

To obtain permission(s) to use material from this work,
please submit a written request to:
SDP Publishing
Permissions Department
PO Box 26, East Bridgewater, MA 02333
or email your request to info@SDPPublishing.com.

Library of Congress Control Number: 2017951982
ISBN-13 (print): 978-0-9984240-5-7
ISBN-13 (ebook): 978-0-9984240-6-4
Printed in the United States of America

©2017 SDG Direct, Ltd. All rights reserved.
Barnicle and Husk™, Barnicle and Husk are trademarks of SDG Direct, Ltd.

DEDICATION

For my loving husband Jim and for
Mom and Dad, whom I deeply miss.

1

The Arrival

All it took for Barnicle the cat to sneak aboard the ship was a short leap, two left turns, a scamper, and a **slither.**

Barnicle slipped behind some wooden crates on the lower deck, hidden from the human passengers. "Finally! I'm on my way," he said, as he licked a paw and smoothed back his whiskers. September 6, 1620 was a good day to start a new adventure.

Once on board, Barnicle learned that this was the third time the *Mayflower* had left **port** for the **New World**. In previous attempts, the ship they were supposed to sail alongside, the *Speedwell*, took on water. After six weeks, the crew sent the *Speedwell* back to port. The *Mayflower* sailed alone.

Barnicle had been sneaking on ships for years. He knew how to quickly find all the best hiding spots. He had sailed around the world on ships carrying everything from tar and lumber to grains and spices. But he loved fishing boats the most. Luscious fish! Barnicle smacked his lips.

Unfortunately, the *Mayflower* was not a fishing boat, but a **cargo ship**. On this trip, though, there would also be passengers, bound for the New World. The passengers, called **Pilgrims**, were originally from England. Some of them had lived in the Netherlands for almost 12 years. They were leaving their home countries because they believed they were losing their freedom to worship as they wished. As for Barnicle, he was leaving England behind to look for new adventures.

Barnicle watched as the Pilgrims waved goodbye to their friends and families who stood on the dock. Barnicle had no friends because he liked to travel alone and do as he pleased. He watched family members dab tears from their eyes as the ship took their loved ones away. He wondered what it was like to be missed by someone.

The *Mayflower* set out across the **Atlantic Ocean** carrying 102 passengers of all ages, a crew of brave sailors, chickens, sheep, some dogs, oodles of mice, and one mischievous feline.

Once the ship had finally left the shores of England, the passengers were already very tired from the long delay. As they rested, Barnicle explored.

Barnicle knew some days the waters and wind on the sea were steady and calm and some days were rocky and rough. It had been several weeks since the *Mayflower* had left England and Barnicle moved around as he pleased, sneaking scraps of food when he could. Every night he went back to his spot on the lower deck behind the crates.

One day, the seas were rougher than normal.

The ship pitched up and down, over huge ocean swells, creaking and groaning as it was tossed by the sea. Barnicle dug his claws into the wooden planks and told his stomach to hold steady. He had been in storms before and knew there was nothing to do but hunker down.

"Oohh," moaned a teensy-tiny voice from somewhere in the shadows. Barnicle's ears perked up. "All this rocking . . . "

Barnicle peeked out from his hiding place.

"Oohh," the voice whimpered again.

He moved slowly toward the voice.

"You there!" Barnicle said in a low, mean growl

to the crying mouse. "This is my spot. Go find somewhere else to moan and be sick."

"Please," cried the mouse, who hid inside a wooden crate, peeking out through a deep crack. "I can't."

"If you can't handle the high seas then you should have stayed on solid ground," Barnicle said. "Now run along before I eat you." His stomach did not feel well from the pitch of the waves, but he was not about to let this little mouse know that.

The mouse poked her nose out of the crack with caution. She sniffed around and then squeezed out of the hole.

"Please don't," she began. Without any warning, the boat lurched far to one side. The mouse tumbled and rolled. When the boat settled, everything and everyone was in a heap, including the mouse. She had landed upside down in a tight little ball right next to Barnicle.

"Hello, mouse," he said. He licked his lips.

"No! I beg you!" she said. "Please don't hurt me."

Something about the plump little mouse's squeaky voice and big eyes made Barnicle stop. He found himself chuckling at her upside-down position.

She untangled herself and sat upright, straightening her dress. She did not like being laughed at. "My name is Agnes," she said. "Not *mouse*." The boat lurched again, and Agnes clutched her tummy. She was very seasick.

Barnicle eyed her up and down. "You sure look healthy for nearly two months at sea, *Agnes*."

"Hardly," said Agnes in a high-pitched squeak.

He looked at her more closely and realized that her tummy was big, but her fur was dirty and matted. Her eyes looked tired and sad.

"Well, Agnes," he said, "you are in luck because I already ate." He patted his belly as if it were full and not rumbling from days of hunger. "I won't be eating you. Not today anyway."

Agnes breathed a sigh of relief. "Thank you, cat."

"Barnicle's the name. Here." He tossed her a

small scrap of bread he had planned to eat later. "I'm so full I can't eat another bite," Barnicle lied. "Might help settle your stomach. How did you end up here anyway?"

Agnes nibbled the bread. "By accident," she said. "I was searching for food inside a crate on the pier when the lid fell shut. Then the crate was moved onto the boat, and I was trapped. The first big storm

we hit sent the crate sliding into the hull. It cracked just enough for me to slip out. I've been hiding here ever since." She took another bite of bread. Barnicle was right—it was helping her stomach.

"Well, I suppose you can stay here," Barnicle said. "But only because you're small and don't take up much space."

So Barnicle and Agnes lived side by side on the lower deck. As the days went by, Barnicle became more concerned about Agnes's health. She looked frail and didn't speak much. He decided to help his little friend and went about the boat looking for anything that might comfort her.

"I found this," Barnicle said, handing her a blond-colored square. "It might help settle your stomach."

"What is it?" Agnes asked as she took the hard biscuit.

"Called hardtack. It's like a cracker. They're everywhere on this ship. I guess they never go rotten. It's a little dry, but it'll get you through the night."

On another night, Agnes felt a little better so she

went with Barnicle to search for new scraps of food, like bits of cheese and salted beef.

Barnicle always made sure to stay in the shadows when he went out on his nightly strolls.

"We're not supposed to be here," he told Agnes as they crept along. "If anyone sees us, there might be a panic."

As they looked for food and fresh water to drink, they spotted two young boys playing.

"What's that they're holding?" Agnes asked.

The two boys laughed and held a long straw-like reed.

"Hold it steady, Francis," one boy said.

"I'm trying, John. This boat is rocking too much," the other said.

Barnicle looked closely at the boys and what they were doing. He noticed a small barrel marked GUN POWDER. When Barnicle saw what the boys were trying to do, his heart began to race.

"I hope they're not . . . "

But Barnicle didn't get a chance to finish his

sentence. A flickering light flew from the end of the **squib** the boy held. He panicked and dropped it onto the deck. Barnicle knew from all his travels on boats that one of the biggest dangers on the sea was a fire aboard a ship.

Agnes gasped and grabbed for Barnicle, but he was already on the move. Not caring that the boys might see him, Barnicle sprang across the wooden planks as the ignited squib rolled closer to the barrel marked GUN POWDER. Barnicle slapped the spewing sparks until he was sure they were extinguished.

"Ow! Burns! Ouch!" Barnicle gasped, blowing on his front paw.

The boys screamed. Agnes wasn't sure what scared them—the fire or the cat jumping out of the shadows. Either way they turned and ran off into the darkness. Agnes raced over to Barnicle.

"Are you okay?" she asked.

Barnicle's paw ached, but he didn't want to worry

Agnes. "Just a little burn. No big deal."

He tried to hide his limp as they searched for food and fresh water. When Barnicle found some water, he dipped his paw in it instead of drinking it.

The ship finally landed at the **Wampanoag** village of **Patuxet,** later called New **Plimoth**, on a cold December morning after a brief stay behind the tip of **Cape Cod**. The long voyage was over. Agnes hoped to find a barn or field, something that would remind her of her faraway home in England.

The ship was anchored a ways off from the shore. Some of the Pilgrim men boarded a small boat called a **shallop** and rowed onto the shore. Barnicle and Agnes had to be very sneaky about getting a ride.

Barnicle saw a tool crate that was open at the top.

"Come on, Agnes," he said, slinking toward it. "Hop in!"

They hid there until the shallop reached the shore and everyone got off. The moment the crate was set down again, Barnicle and Agnes quickly ducked behind a large rock until everyone was out of sight. Walking was very difficult since their legs were like jelly from many months at sea.

"You okay?" Barnicle asked Agnes.

She nodded. "I just need a moment."

Barnicle looked out at the sea they had survived, and back toward the land where new adventures waited. With his sharp claw he carved into the rock Agnes leaned against.

"What are you doing?" Agnes asked.

"Making my mark," he said. Agnes watched as he wrote BARNICLE WAS HERE 1620.

"Barnicle . . ."

"It's fine," he said as he inspected his work. The paw print on the "i" of his name was his signature trick.

"No, it's not," Agnes said. "You spelled your own name wrong."

"No I didn't," he said, bristling. "I think I know how to spell my own name, thank you very much."

"Your name is spelled B-a-r-n-a-c-l-e. It's an 'a', not an 'i'." Agnes shook her head.

"Well . . . I know that," Barnicle said. "I . . . I write it this way on purpose. Because it's different. Like me."

Agnes managed a smile. "You *are* different, Barnicle. That's what I like about you."

"Are you sure you will be okay?" Barnicle asked.

They had already talked about going their separate ways once the ship landed. He planned to start a new adventure, but Agnes wanted to stay in one place.

"Yes, I'll be fine," she said.

Barnicle began to understand how all those tearful people on the pier back in England felt, waving goodbye to those they cared about. He would miss Agnes.

She walked away from the rock on weak legs. Barnicle had taken care of her for long enough. Agnes was sure he'd be glad to get rid of her. "Don't worry about me," she said. "I plan to find myself a nice field to lay in while the sun shines down on me."

Still, she looked frail and the weather was cold.

He gave her a gentle hug goodbye. "Take care," he said. And then he added, "Friend."

Agnes grinned. "Go find new places to explore, my friend."

2

Husk

Agnes waddled off toward the woods. She was eager to rest in a nice patch of grass. As she walked away, she stopped one last time to turn back to look at Barnicle.

Barnicle had stopped too. They waved to each other again. Agnes felt a heaviness in her stomach that had nothing to do with the secret she kept inside.

"Don't worry, little one," she said as she rubbed her belly. "I will find the perfect home for you before you are born." It was almost time, and Agnes was ready to rest.

She searched about for just the right place to have her baby. She needed somewhere that was soft and warm, safe and peaceful. When she found the perfect spot in a cornfield near a pond, she snuggled down among the fallen corn husks and waited.

After a few long, shivery days, Agnes gave birth to a tiny boy mouse. Even though she was tired and weak, she was the happiest she had ever been as she held her baby in her arms.

"You will be safe here," she promised her son. She

nestled him into the softness of the fluffy corn silk. Her heart had never felt so full and happy. "Your tuft of fur looks just like the silk," she said. She kissed his tiny head.

She tucked him into a cornhusk and carefully folded the edges to keep him warm. She smiled at her perfect little bundle. "I will call you Husk," she told him. "And I'll love you always."

Each night, with the silence of the fields surrounding them, Agnes told Husk stories of her home on the farm and her long trip across the Atlantic Ocean.

"At first I was all alone on that big rollicking ship," she told Husk. His wide eyes looked up at her in wonder. "I had you in my belly and the ship kept swaying back and forth, again and again. I had nothing to eat, but the seas were so violent, I wasn't sure I could keep any food down. One day, a cat with orange stripes appeared. I thought he might eat me," she said, with a small laugh at the memory. "Instead, he saved my life—and yours, Husk. He brought me food to eat and kept me warm and hidden from the passengers."

She tucked the cornhusk tighter around his shoulders. Husk drifted off to sleep, dreaming of cats with orange stripes.

As the days went on, Agnes became thinner and weaker. She did not want her son to know how sick she was. She tried to make sure he had enough food to last him a little while. Still, every night she told Husk stories, hoping that he would remember.

"Good night, my sweet boy," she said one night. She had just finished another story, and kissed Husk on the head like she always did.

Then Agnes put her head down, gasped her last breath, and never woke up again.

Little Husk was now on his own—hungry, cold, and scared. He missed his mother. What was he going to do without her? How would he survive? Although his mother had left him food, winter had arrived and Husk knew he would soon have to fend for himself. Even though he was scared, he headed out into the fields to find food.

Husk searched for a long time, but found nothing in the cold winter landscape. He wandered aimlessly until he realized with a fright that he was lost. He didn't know where he was or how to get back to his warm little home. Suddenly, a sharp-clawed hawk

circled above him, screeching and swooping. The hawk swooped closer and closer to Husk, who ran in zigzag patterns to avoid being attacked. His heart pounded and tears filled his eyes. He whimpered for his mother. He was sure he'd never survive.

3

Running Deer

Luck was on Husk's side that day. The hawk did not capture him. Instead, a young girl heard his tiny cries. She searched through the fields, lifting dried leaves and pushing aside the withered cornstalks. She also kept a close eye on the hawk, watching his every movement. She knew that whatever the hawk was after was close by.

At last she discovered a shivering field mouse hiding inside a rotted ear of corn.

"Are you okay, little one?" she asked, bending close to see him. Husk backed away. "It's okay. I won't hurt you."

Husk looked up at the girl. She didn't look like she would hurt him. Her face was open and kind

and she had big brown eyes. "I . . . I'm okay," he said, even though his heart still raced.

"What's your name?" the girl asked. She wore her straight dark hair in long braids, and around her neck was a necklace of shells strung on a leather string.

"My name is Husk."

"That's a nice name," she said. "Like from the

corn we eat, right?"

"Yes," said Husk. "My mother gave me the name."

"She must be a very clever mother. Where is she? Did you get lost?"

"My mother is gone," Husk said, his eyes filling with tears. "I have to look for food on my own now, but I went too far and now I am lost." Husk shivered in the cold air. He was sure his tears would freeze right on his face.

"Poor little mouse! Don't worry. You can come live with me in my village. Would you like that?"

Husk didn't know what to say, but he nodded.

"I'll show you my **wetu**," she added, but Husk did not know what a wetu was. He was just happy that she was so kind. "My name is Running Deer."

"Hello," Husk finally managed to say. "Thank you for helping me."

"Of course," she said. "Ready to go for a little ride?"

Running Deer carefully plucked Husk from the ground and put him in a pouch of soft deerskin that was attached to her belt.

"This is a wetu?" he asked.

She laughed gently. "No, this is my pouch, and here is some **parched corn** for you to nibble on. Have some, if you're hungry."

Husk didn't think he could get any luckier than this. He was warm and safe and had food to eat. Running Deer had saved his life.

"Are you comfortable? Warm?" she asked.

"Very," Husk said. The pouch was as warm as his mother's comforting hugs. He felt snug and safe inside. Whatever a wetu was, he was sure he'd like it very much.

Running Deer started off through the woods, stepping rhythmically. The rocking soon made Husk drift off to sleep.

4

The Wampanoag

The first thing Husk noticed as he slowly woke from the warmth and safety of Running Deer's pouch was the smell—a woodsy scent of what could only be cooking fires burning. He thought of how warm he was, but being next to a fire seemed just as cozy.

"Wake up, Husk," Running Deer said. "We're almost home." She opened the pouch. The winter sun shined down on his face.

Husk peeked out. A busy village hummed and buzzed with life as people bustled to and fro.

"Is this your family?" Husk asked. He was amazed that so many people might be a part of one family.

Running Deer laughed. "Some are, yes. But in some ways we are all family because we live and work together on the land **Kiehtan**, our Creator, made."

But Husk was very nervous. He had only ever known his mother, and now she was gone. "What if they don't like me?"

"They will love you," she promised.

Husk looked at the people around him. Men were dressed in warm animal skin clothes talking to one another as women cooked over the fires. Children helped with chores, like grinding corn, or raced each other around the village.

"What are those?" Husk asked of one of the many round structures he saw people coming in and out of.

"Those are the wetus I told you about," Running Deer said. "They are the homes we live in."

"They look so cozy," Husk said. Spirals of smoke drifted out of some of them. He watched the smoke swirl up into the sky.

"They keep us very warm, especially in the winter," she said. "They are made of saplings covered with large sheets of bark and lined with woven bulrush-reed mats."

"So you don't have to sleep on the snowy ground?"

"The wetus keep us warm and dry," she said. "These are my people. We are the Wampanoag."

Husk couldn't help but notice how proud she was as she looked about the village.

Everyone looked happy working together, and there was a feeling of peace in the village. Husk decided this must be a wonderful place to live.

"How long have you lived here?" he asked Running Deer.

"Thousands of years." Husk's eyes widened. Running Deer laughed. "Not me personally, but my ancestors have been here for that long. See right down there?" She pointed down a path, where light shone. "That's east toward the water. The first light of the day shines down there. That's why we are called the **People of the First Light**. Come on, I'll introduce you to my family."

Husk was excited but nervous to meet so many new people. He worried that they would not welcome him as kindly as Running Deer had. Maybe they didn't want someone new living in their village.

"Don't worry," she said. She scooped him out of her pouch and gave him a hug. "They will love you."

Husk followed her into one of the wetus, the home where Running Deer's family lived together.

He didn't need to worry. Running Deer's family welcomed him. He met her mother, sister, grandmother, and grandfather.

"This is my new friend, Husk," she said. "He was lost, frightened, and all alone. I found him just in time, before the hawk made a meal out of him." Husk looked at Running Deer gratefully.

"Don't you have a blanket or something warm for your feet?" her mother asked Husk. She had a very worried look on her face.

"No," he said. Husk thought of the cornhusk his mother had wrapped him in.

"We will take care of that," she said. With that, they wrapped a warm painted **hide** around him to keep away the winter chill.

That first night, Husk snuggled into the pouch he had arrived in which made a very cozy bed. As everyone drifted off to sleep, Running Deer reached over and lightly stroked the top of his head. Soon, Husk fell asleep.

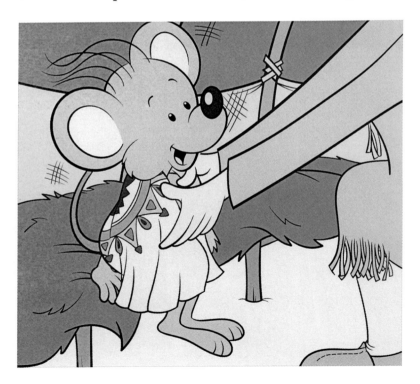

5

Village Life

Days in the village started early and stayed busy. Running Deer taught important lessons about food gathering and the seasons.

"Each season, we prepare for the next," she explained one afternoon as Husk listened closely. Her little sister, Winonna, stood with them.

Husk looked around. "But how?" He stomped the ground with his tiny foot. "Even the ground is frozen."

"Winter is when we rest," Running Deer said. "The river is frozen and the food we hunted and gathered is stored here, in these baskets." She showed him where the village's food was stored. "Down there, see?" She pointed.

Husk pulled back the woven mat and saw the baskets of food placed deep in the ground below the frost line.

"That way the food will last until the warmer months of planting time."

"Planting time," Husk repeated. "What's that?"

"I know!" Winonna said, jumping up and down, eager to answer. Running Deer smiled and smoothed down her sister's hair.

"Go ahead, tell him."

"It's when we plant seeds in the ground that grow into food!" she said.

"That's right," Running Deer said.

"Corn and squash and beans and pumpkins and sunflowers and watermelons . . . "

"Okay, Winonna. I think he gets the point," Running Deer laughed.

"Will I get to plant the seeds too?" Husk asked.

"I always help with the planting," she said. "But a big, strong mouse like you? I think you should help the men."

Running Deer probably didn't know it, but that made Husk feel very grown up.

"The men and boys hunt," Winonna explained. She held up her arms in front of her. "*Whoosh!* They use their bows and arrows to hunt and fish. And they protect the whole entire village."

"A very important job," Running Deer agreed. "Do you think you are up to the task?"

Husk nodded eagerly. He wanted to be just like the Wampanoag!

Overhearing the discussion, one of the elders, named Flying Eagle, said to Husk, "When we hunt, we do not waste any part of the animal. Sinew, or tendons that connect muscle and bone, is made into string. Even parts of the fish we catch can be used as fertilizer for the crops we grow."

One day, when the weather turned a bit warmer, some of the men took Husk out to fish in **mishoons** they had made themselves from chestnut and pine trees.

As Flying Eagle gazed out at the calm morning waters, he asked Husk, "What of your family?"

Husk still felt very sad about his mother, but the Wampanoag had been so kind and loving to him that he felt like one of their family. He was grateful to have them.

"My mother died when I was very young," Husk said. "She gave me my name and told me stories."

Flying Eagle nodded. "Stories are a very important part of our culture as well. Stories tell us where we come from. Where did your mother come from?"

"She arrived on a big ship from a place called England. She said the journey was long and hard." She had also once told Husk that she had loved him before she'd even seen him, but he did not tell Flying Eagle that.

Husk learned that the food they hunted for was abundant around their village. Deer, wild turkey, raccoon, rabbit, skunk, bear, and beaver were some of the animals they hunted and survived on. What

they didn't eat right away they dried and stored in the baskets in the ground.

As the warm season arrived, all the families moved to their summer wetus along the shore. New tasks began as planting ceremonies were done to begin the summer. The nearby river's fresh water brought a bounty of fish, and the ocean close by rewarded them with other kinds of fish.

Sometimes Husk went with the men in mishoons when they fished. Where the rivers emptied into the ocean, shellfish, such as clams, mussels, oysters, and **quahogs** were plentiful. Other times he went with the women into the woods to gather berries, nuts, and plants that could be used for medicinal purposes and teas. Husk watched with wonder as the women taught Running Deer how to fashion pots from clay and weave mats of reeds. Each person had a task; everyone pitched in.

No one was ever bored because there was always something different to do.

6
Lessons Learned

It had been a full year since Husk had joined Running Deer and the Wampanoag people in their village. He loved working with the others to keep the village running smoothly—he had learned so many new skills! His favorite part about life in the village, though, was listening to the elders tell stories of Wampanoag history. The stories were lessons of life, wisdom of past generations, and history back to the time of Creation.

"We must never forget the time long ago," the messenger sent by **Massasoit** began.

Running Deer sat and listened to the messenger, as Husk leaned in closer, eager to hear the stories of her people. He learned of the disease that had recently swept through their villages and killed thousands of Wampanoag people.

"Many years ago, some of our people were stolen from our own land and taken across the seas. Stolen from us, their home, their families."

Running Deer trembled, her eyes tearfully wide as she listened to the story of her people. She remembered the piercing screams the day her

father, brother, and the others were taken, when Running Deer was a small child. Her attention drifted from the story, and she found herself distracted by the last image of her father. He stretched his hand out as she tried to grab it with her own. But the invaders pushed him to the ground, bound him, and dragged him away. He never returned.

Husk listened intently to every word. That night he stayed close to Running Deer. He wasn't sure if he was comforting her or if it was the other way around.

Husk liked being in the wetu with Running Deer. He thought about everything the messenger had told them.

Upset by the stories Husk had learned of Running Deer's family, he had difficulty falling asleep. He only wished he could have helped. Once asleep, he dreamt of being a fierce protector and hunter like he thought Running Deer's friend Pathfinder was. Upon waking, Husk excitedly told Running Deer of his dream. "I crept along silently and found my prey and *wham!* Food for everyone!"

Running Deer chuckled, "I'm sure you would be a good hunter, however, you are a mouse." Husk sighed.

Running Deer explained to Husk that before the hunt, we pray for the animal that is giving up its life. Animals should not be taken for granted, and we are to give thanks for the food they have provided us.

Just then, Pathfinder came into the wetu and plopped down on a fur blanket. They were good friends, and he often told her and Husk about his adventures in the woods.

"You should have seen it," he said. He took a drink of water from the gourd bottle near the fire. "We were all behind a log, rabbit in our sights. I pulled back my arrow like this," Pathfinder motioned with his arms, "and just before I let go, Little Bear sneezes and off runs the rabbit."

Running Deer laughed, but Husk wondered if he could be perfectly silent on a hunt.

"Little Bear couldn't sneak up on a pile of bones without spooking it," Running Deer said. "He's always tripping over branches and stubbing his toe on rocks."

"Would you like to follow us on our next hunt?" Pathfinder asked Husk. "Do you think you can keep up?"

"Yes!" Husk said without thinking. He wanted to be just like Pathfinder.

"We run for miles," he warned. "Have you ever

been on a deer trail? There are many briars and thickets. They can be tricky, so you have to keep up."

"I can do it!" Husk stood up, bouncing on his little feet.

"Make sure you tell him the biggest rule," Running Deer said.

"You have to be patient," Pathfinder said.

"I will be!"

"Fast and strong," Pathfinder said.

"I promise I'll keep up."

"But most importantly," said Pathfinder, "*no noise*. Silence is as important as our aim. If we make any noise, our prey will disappear, and the hunt is over."

"Got it."

"Watch where you step. Don't step on dried leaves. You will scare the deer or rabbit and off they will run. Can you do it?"

"I'll be as quiet as a mouse," Husk said earnestly.

Husk was so excited the day the boys took him out on their hunt.

"We follow the tracks the animals leave. See?" Pathfinder pointed to hoof marks in the soft earth. "And these broken branches mean he's gone that way."

Husk and the others followed Pathfinder through the woods. Husk tried to mimic the smooth way Pathfinder walked. One of the boys snickered when Husk held his arms up as if he had his very own bow and arrow.

Husk could not yet keep up with the long, fast

distances that the other boys traveled, but Pathfinder gladly tucked him into his deerskin pouch.

They returned that day without any game. The men, however, arrived back in the village with a large deer.

"For your first time out," Pathfinder told him, "you did great."

"We must always give thanks," Pathfinder added.

"Kiehtan created these lands and made them full and bountiful."

One day, Pathfinder told Husk of a very important time in every Wampanoag boy's life.

"Soon I will go off on my own," he said. "Perhaps for several months."

"But why?" Husk asked. He didn't want Pathfinder to leave.

"Each boy must prove he can survive alone under all conditions. But don't worry, little one." He playfully nudged Husk. "When I return, I will have learned many things and grown into a man who can help protect his family."

7

Cat Burglar

One night as everyone slept, Husk heard a rustling outside.

He slipped out from his pouch. He quietly peeked out the door as his heart pounded. The moon was so full and bright it cast a shadow against the wetu. He thought he saw something move.

"I must be brave, I must be brave," he whispered to himself. He had learned to be courageous from observing his Wampanoag friends. Now was the time to prove it.

He stepped outside. There was nothing there. Had he imagined the sound?

An odd noise came from the edge of the wetus where the food was stored. Husk listened closely.

"Mmm . . . yumm . . . mmm . . ."

He got closer and realized a creature had dug into their food supply!

Husk's paws shook as he tiptoed toward the thief, his heart racing.

"Stop!" he said. "Who are you? Why are you eating our food?"

The thief was a scrawny orange cat. He didn't

budge. The greedy beast took a big piece of fish. "So you caught me," he said. "Now what?" As if answering his own question, he took a big bite out of the fish.

"Well, I . . . I . . . " Husk stammered. It made him angry to see this animal eating the food his friends had worked hard to grow and hunt. But what was he going to do about it?

"It's cold and I'm starving," the cat sighed. "No one will miss a tiny bit of fish." The cat took another bite.

"Stop!" Husk said. "That's stealing." Husk no longer felt afraid. He felt angry at this bully cat for taking their food.

"Oh, relax," the cat said. Husk refused to back down. "Fine, I'll stop eating." He put the remainder of the fish back where he had found it. "Happy?"

Husk moved closer. "Who are you?" he demanded.

The cat stretched his long thin body. "Barnicle's the name."

Husk nearly fell over. He looked closely at the thief. Orange. Stripes. Cat. Barnicle.

"H-how did you get here?" Husk asked.

"I walked," he said. "How else?"

"No, I mean . . . did you . . . sail here?" Husk felt silly asking the question but he needed to know for sure.

"Why do you ask, mouse?" the cat said. He squinted at Husk. "Do I know you?"

"No, but I think you knew my mother." The cat watched him closely. "She came here on a ship called the *Mayflower*. Her name was Agnes."

Barnicle slowly sat up, his eyes wide. He looked closely at Husk. A moment ago he had thought what a tasty meal the mouse would be. Now, with Agnes's name being mentioned after so long, he knew he couldn't do it. Still, the mouse didn't need to know that. Not yet, anyway.

"What's your name, boy?"

"I am not a boy anymore. And my name is Husk. I live here in the Wampanoag village."

"But your mother . . . your mother is Agnes?"

Husk nodded yes, thoughts of his mother racing

through his mind. "She told me about you. How you helped her on the boat crossing the sea from England. I was born soon after she arrived."

"And then?"

"And then," Husk said, tears stinging his eyes, "she died."

Barnicle slumped against one of the food baskets. "Agnes . . . your mother . . . was wonderful. Sweet and fearless and determined to stay healthy—for you."

They sat quietly for a moment, each thinking his own thoughts. She was missed very much.

"Maybe I could share *some* of this fish with you," Husk offered. He knew Running Deer and the Wampanoag would share their food with new friends. He also knew his mother would be proud of the kind gesture.

Barnicle smacked his lips. "Don't mind if I do. Thanks . . . Husk."

The two sat for hours, nibbling on fish and corn and telling their stories.

Husk told Barnicle how Running Deer found him and took him into her village and family. "She and her people have taught me everything I know," he said. "I wouldn't have survived that first winter without them."

"The kindness you showed me tonight," Barnicle said, "is from your mother. She was the kindest creature I ever met. She refused to let me take any food from the children on board the ship, even if it had fallen to the ground. 'They need it more than we do,' she always said."

"When she told me about you," Husk said, "she said you were the most adventurous creature she had ever met. Is it true you once sailed on a ship with pirates across a sea with clear waters?"

"The **Caribbean**, yes!" Barnicle said. "Rough journey, that was. The ship I hid on was attacked no less than three times. Never found me, though! Stayed hidden just like that chest of gold they held."

"Really?" Husk asked in disbelief. "Where did you hide?"

Barnicle leaned close to Husk and said, "Right behind the treasure chest."

Husk looked at Barnicle carefully. "Is that a true story?"

"Of course," Barnicle said with a wave of his paw. "The best part about the Caribbean is the tuna." He smacked his lips. "Best tuna I ever had."

They talked until the sun began to rise over the village.

Barnicle had lost a friend and companion in Agnes, but gained a new friend in Husk. As for Husk, he had learned so many lessons from the Wampanoag.

8

A Start to a Great Adventure

The sun's first light peeked from the horizon and cast a warm glow over the Wampanoag village. As they watched the sky brighten on a brand-new day, Barnicle asked Husk a serious question.

"Do you want to join me as I go back out to explore the world?"

The question surprised Husk, who had never thought about leaving Running Deer and the Wampanoag, though the stories of his mother's travels had always stayed with him.

He thought about how much of the world there was to see—so many places he could hardly imagine it all. He thought of Pathfinder, who he had watched go off on his own to become a man. Everyone in the village had taught Husk everything he knew. He didn't realize until Barnicle asked him the question how much he had grown, and how curious he was about the world.

"Yes," Husk finally said. "I do!"

"Are you sure?" Barnicle asked. "Life can be hard when you are always on the move, from one place to the next. I'll be there, but you have to be able to take care of yourself."

"I'm ready," Husk said, and he meant it. As much as he loved his adopted family, he was ready to strike out on his own like Pathfinder. "It's time for me to prove that I can survive whatever comes my way."

That very morning, Husk told Running Deer about his plans.

"I'm so proud of you," Running Deer said. That surprised Husk, but also made him feel warm and loved. "You are strong and smart. You're ready to see the world. I'll miss you very much, though."

Husk hugged Running Deer. "Thank you for everything," he said. "Thank you for saving my life."

"We are always here if you ever come back. You'll always have a place among our people."

As Husk gathered his things from the wetu, he knew the Wampanoag people had prepared him well for his future.

"Goodbye," he said, tears forming in his little eyes as he hugged Running Deer one last time. "I promise to come back. I don't know when, but I will."

"You better," she said, smiling through her tears.

"We're going to miss you. I have something for you."
She took out a small deerskin pouch. "I made this
for you."

Husk took the soft pouch in his tiny hands.

"Here, I'll help you put it on," she offered.
Running Deer tied a leather belt around Husk's waist
and attached the pouch to it.

"Thank you. I'll always keep it with me."

"Don't forget about us," she said.

"I could never." As he adjusted his belt he heard
rustling in the pouch.

"Parched corn," Running Deer said. "For
your journey."

Husk gave her one more hug—fearing he'd start
crying again if he held her for more than a quick
moment—and turned to leave the village. With a
wave back to his adopted family, he spotted the hawk
circling high above. Husk was no longer frightened
of him.

Barnicle waited for him at the top of a large
boulder by the shore. He jumped off and grabbed a

small striped rock and handed it to Husk.

"I heard these were lucky! Are you ready for whatever happens next, my friend?"

"Yes, I am," Husk answered.

It was a good day, and the adventure was just beginning.

ATLANTIC OCEAN – The body of water between Europe and the Americas.

CAPE COD – Part of the original territory of the Wampanoag Nation. It is the modern day name for where 41 English colonists signed the *Mayflower Compact* on November 11, 1620, in a town called Provincetown, located at the tip of Cape Cod.

CARGO SHIP – A ship that carries goods and materials.

CARIBBEAN – Body of water that is an arm of the Atlantic bounded on the north and east by the West Indies, on the south by South America, and on the west by Central America, and connected with the Gulf of Mexico by the Yucatán Channel.

HIDE – Animal skin, whether raw or prepared, for human use.

IMMIGRATION – The act of coming to a foreign place to live. The Pilgrims immigrated to Patuxet (now referred to as Plymouth, where the Wampanoag have lived for over 10,000 years) from England and the Netherlands. The Pilgrims did not settle in an empty wilderness, but within the territory of the Wampanoag Nation.

KIEHTAN – The name of the Creator in Wampanoag tradition.

MAYFLOWER – A cargo ship that took the Pilgrims to the New World.

MASSASOIT – Means "great leader." His name was Ousamequin.

MISHOON – The Wampanoag word for boat. They are made from several types of wood (logs) and hollowed out by burning, and then scraping the charred wood out to shape the boat. The charred wood is softer and easier to remove than the green wood of a fresh-cut tree.

NEW WORLD – A name for the Americas. European people referred to the Americas as the "New World" during the colonization period in the 1600s.

PARCHED CORN – Dried corn kernels that are roasted in a pan or kettle, and then ground into meal. This parched corn meal was called "Nokehick." Men would carry it in pouches worn around the waist when they were hunting or traveling.

PATUXET – This is the Wampanoag name for the place the Pilgrims settled that was later called Plymouth. Patuxet was one of 69 original villages of the Wampanoag Nation, and of many that were wiped out in a great plague between 1616 and 1618.

PEOPLE OF THE FIRST LIGHT – The word "Wampanoag" means "People of the First Light." This refers to the fact that they live on the east coast where the sun rises.

PILGRIM – Wanderer or traveler to a foreign place. Early settlers that traveled from Europe to what is now Plymouth, Massachusetts.

PLIMOTH – The old spelling of "Plymouth," used by Governor William Bradford. Plimoth Plantation, the living history museum in Plymouth, MA, uses this particular spelling to differentiate itself from the modern town of Plymouth, MA.

PORT – A place alongside a coast where ships load and unload.

QUAHOG – A thick-shelled, edible clam.

SACHEM – The chief of a village.

SHALLOP – A small boat stored below the decks, reassembled for launch from the *Mayflower*, which carried the Pilgrims from the *Mayflower* to the shore.

SLITHER – To slip or slide like a snake.

SPEEDWELL – The ship that was meant to sail alongside the *Mayflower*, but was sent back to port twice for leaks that could not be repaired.

SQUIB – A straw-like tube filled with gunpowder, generally used to ignite a charge.

WAMPANOAG – The Native or original people of what is now Southeastern Massachusetts and surrounding areas. They have resided in this area for over 10,000 years.

WETU – The Wampanoag word for "house." The traditional homes were dome-shaped buildings with a frame made of saplings (young trees). During the summer, they were covered in cattail mats, and in the winter they were covered in bark.

IMPACT STATEMENT

RESPONSIBILITY OF AUTHORS

When an author uses a culture that is not their own as a vehicle to tell a story, they have certain responsibilities to that culture. This is true for any culture, but in the story of *Barnicle and Husk™*, it is the Wampanoag people and culture that are the setting for this first story.

The author and team have worked very hard to ensure the following things were considered in the representations of Wampanoag people, culture and history in *Barnicle and Husk.*

Authors should take responsibility:

1. To ensure that the culture be represented in a manner that aligns with the way the people of the culture want to be represented — the way they see themselves. That is the truth of those people.

2. Not to alter the culture for any purpose, as this can create or perpetuate stereotypes, misconceptions or distortions. It does not matter if a story is fiction or non-fiction — no one has the right to create a false image of someone's culture.

- Stereotypes, misconceptions, and distortions are images, thoughts, beliefs or representations of a people that are not true, accurate or appropriate to the actual culture.

In the case of the Wampanoag (and all Native Americans), stereotypes, misconceptions, and distortions have led other people to have wrong information or have erroneous beliefs.

For example, other people sometimes believe that

- Wampanoag people do not exist anymore

- That we come from a "backward" or "primitive" culture, not as advanced or sophisticated (not as good as) as European or modern cultures

- That we are no longer "real" Indians

None of the above three points are true. But, when other people believe such things, they are believing something that is wrong. They believe the wrong thing is right or true.

- This is harmful to them because they are carrying and believing falsehoods about other people, especially if their words, written or spoken, or their actions are guided by those falsehoods.

- The people of the culture are hurt by such wrong beliefs/words/actions because it places them in positions to constantly have to explain, defend, or justify themselves as Wampanoag or Native people to other people. No one should have to defend themselves in terms of their nationality or culture. When such a situation happens, there is no equality.

  - For example, many Wampanoag people, as children, have had the experience of being told by an adult that they were not really Indian. The adult (teacher or other) is therefore denying who that child is, and is countering everything else the child has learned in their home and community. This is a very confusing, humiliating, and hurtful experience for a child. It is damaging to their self-esteem to hear such things consistently over years of time. The adult in such a case does not have the right to tell the child who they are or are not. (combined these into one "example")

- To preserve a culture's integrity and present it in an appropriate manner is to show respect for the culture and the people of it, and to therefore engender respect in the reader of the story.

HISTORICAL IMPACTS IN THE
BARNICLE AND HUSK STORY

Two very significant events in Wampanoag history are mentioned in the story. They both happened before the Pilgrims arrived in 1620, and yet their impact lingers with the Wampanoag people today.

The first mention was when Running Deer's father and brother were stolen away, never to be heard from again. In the first years of the 1600's, there were several European ship captains who in sailing up and down the East coast, stopped and kidnapped men from Wampanoag and other coastal people. They enticed men on board the ships under the guise of trading, but would lift anchor and sail away to England. The Wampanoag men were sold into slavery in England and in Spain, or were paraded through the streets of cities like London as "novelties."

Wampanoag or other Native people could be considered "novelties" as we were not Christians, and those who were not Christian were considered to be less than human. Most of these Wampanoag men that were taken literally just disappeared one day, never to be seen or heard from again. Their families and loved ones had to learn to cope with their loss, and the impact that made on their lives.

There are only two known men who made it back from Europe, and survived to tell the tale. The first person everyone has most likely heard of: a man named Tisquantum, better known as Squanto. Tisquantum was from the village of Patuxet, which is where the Pilgrims settled and later renamed Plimoth. He was captured in 1614, and after 5 years managed to find a ship to bring him home in 1619. During his time in England, he learned to speak English, and that is what made him such a valuable ally to the Pilgrims. Tisquantum died in 1622.

The second man was Epanow from the village of Aquinnah on Noepe, now Martha's Vineyard Island. He was captured in 1611, taken to England, and was marched through the streets of London as a "novelty." However, as Epanow came to learn English, he also learned what the English people were most interested in obtaining from their explorations to America: gold. He told them that there were gold mines on Noepe, and if they brought him home, he would lead them to the mines. They did in fact bring him back to Aquinnah in 1614, but Epanow jumped ship when they got close to shore, and successfully made his escape. Epanow lived a long life and became the sachem or chief of his community.

The other historical event mentioned in the story is the plague, known as "The Great Dying," that struck the East coast between 1616 and 1618. Wampanoag and other Natives who were devastated by this disease knew that it came from European fishermen who were off the coast of Maine. Once the Native people got this disease, it spread rapidly down the coast, wiping out entire villages in its path. The Wampanoag originally had 69 villages in our nation, and in the two-year span lost up to 90% of our entire population. Our estimates put our pre-plague population at 70,000 to 100,000 people, and after the plague, 20,000 to 25,000.

The Wampanoag village of Patuxet, where the Pilgrims settled and renamed Plimoth, was one of the villages that was completely wiped out. The only known survivor was Tisquantum, who ironically lived by virtue of having been kidnapped. As the Pilgrims explored the area, and traveled up the coast on trading expeditions, they passed village after village of broken-down homes, overgrown cornfields, and the bones of the dead bleaching in the sun. So many Wampanoag people got sick and died so quickly, that there was no one to care for them or bury the dead. When people succumbed to the illness, they laid on the ground where they died. The Wampanoag people have never to this day recovered to the point of our original population, and today number approximately 5,000.

While we are small in number compared to our original population, we are still here living our culture and carrying on our traditions. That fact, and how we live our traditional life in today's world, is the truth of our culture. It is how we seek to educate others and raise their awareness of the difference between historical and cultural realities versus stereotypes, misconceptions, and distortions.

Linda Jeffers Coombs
Aquinnah Wampanoag

ABOUT THE CREATOR

Mary Shields is the founder and president of Shields Design Studio. She splits her time between Plymouth, MA, and Harpswell, ME, with her husband Jim McKinnell. She has two grown stepchildren and two beautiful granddaughters.

Creative work was something Mary knew she would continue after she received an honorable award for her painting of an abstract forest fire in first grade. Mary founded Shields Design in 1991 and is located in the historic Plymouth waterfront. Nearly three decades later, Shields Design Studio continues to design visuals, from digital to print, for an impressive clientele ranging from tourism, healthcare, sports, technology, government agencies, and entertainment giants.

The ideas for Barnicle™ and Husk™ percolated in the late 1990s, inspired by Mary's personal life experiences. A chance encounter with Wampanoag Chief Flying Eagle, Earl Mills, Sr., helped her project take wing. His wisdom and encouragement were priceless.

The characters' home in Plymouth is richly steeped in history. The mission of Plymouth 400, Inc. and Mary's vision for her historical characters are well aligned. To learn more about the Plymouth 400th commemoration, visit Plymouth400inc.org. Although the characters are fictional, they're woven into a fabric of reality. Whether you choose to follow them on an adventure for fun, or learn from them, they are sure to capture both the young and the young-at-heart.

Barnicle and Husk will prove to be a multifaceted brand with a pipeline of fun for kids. Visit BARNICLEandHUSK.com!

ABOUT PLYMOUTH 400

Plymouth Colony's 400th anniversary commemorates the 1620 landing of the Pilgrims on Cape Cod, in Plymouth, Massachusetts, and in the cities and towns that expanded as part of Plymouth Colony. The commemoration highlights the cultural contributions and American traditions that began with the interaction of the Wampanoag and English peoples, a story that is still relevant today.

This anniversary is the Nation's most significant to date. It is America's Founding Story and the icon of our national holiday, Thanksgiving. The story, including Native American history and culture and America's immigration story, is inclusive of themes that resonate with people of many cultures.

The Signature events and programs of Plymouth 400 will help to renew awareness among residents and visitors to Massachusetts wishing to learn more about Plymouth County, Cape Cod, Boston and other historic destinations.

"OUR" STORY, 400 YEARS OF WAMPANOAG HISTORY

This unprecedented exhibit, *"Our" Story: 400 Years of Wampanoag History*, reveals little-known historic and cultural realities of the People of the First Light. *"Our" Story: 400 Years of Wampanoag History* is conceptualized, researched, and produced by a team of Wampanoag people of both Aquinnah and Mashpee Plymouth 400's Wampanoag Advisory Committee. The exhibit is part of Plymouth 400, Inc.'s Signature Programs and Events and will continue to travel through 2020. Additional chapters of Wampanoag history will be added each year in November. Inquiries regarding upcoming locations and opportunities for hosting this exhibit should be directed to Plymouth 400, Inc. www.plymouth400inc.org.

ACKNOWLEDGMENTS

I would like to extend my heartfelt thanks to my mentor, Wampanoag Chief Flying Eagle, Earl Mills, Sr., of Mashpee, MA, for all his support. This project may never have taken off without the encouragement and collaboration he kindly offered when I reached out to him. I am thankful for the time Earl spent sharing the stories of his people that expanded my inspiration into something greater than planned. I will continue to use the knowledge he has given me, as well as that of other cultural leaders, to develop a series of children's books based on various aspects of history and culture, using my fictional characters as a vehicle to spark interest. Earl is a leader, educator, entrepreneur, storyteller, and author. Books written include *Son of Mashpee*, *Cape Cod Wampanoag Cookbook*, *Talking with the Elders of Mashpee*, and *Education, Teachers, Activities and More*.

Thank you to Linda Jeffers Coombs for her consultation, patience and guidance throughout my journey. The lessons I have learned through this process have been remarkable. Linda Jeffers Coombs is an Aquinnah Wampanoag and is a Museum Educator and Wampanoag Historian. Linda and I currently serve as Board Members for Plymouth 400, Inc.

And to Plymouth 400, Inc. whose inspiring mission is to plan and execute a 400th anniversary commemoration that is historically accurate, culturally inclusive and which shines a light on America's founding story, renewing its legacy, and preserving it for future generations.

"America is poised for an Anniversary of national and international significance; the 400th Anniversary of the Mayflower *voyage and the founding of Plymouth Colony. The Plymouth 400 Anniversary will highlight the cultural contributions and American traditions*

that began with the interaction of the Wampanoag and English peoples, a story that significantly shaped the building of America."
– Plymouth 400, Inc.

A special thank you to artist Bob Ostrom for creating the images for my dream.

Thank you to Lisa Akoury-Ross who has helped me navigate the publishing world. I am grateful for the guidance she and her team, Taylor Morris and Ashley Fedor, provided throughout the entirety of this process.

I could not have accomplished this without my amazing staff at Shields Design Studio (SDG Direct, Ltd.). The talented team of creative forces, both on staff and freelance, are behind my every move keeping me on course. Whether they are illustrators, designers, developers, or writers, I believe teamwork makes the best product. My vision is amplified and able to be executed with their help. I am truly grateful to Ali Stevenson, Sally McCarthy, Steve Polito, Alyson Gluck, Sheryl Quesnel, Tom Vacchino, Katie Buckell, Nicole Gouthro, Jeff Costa, Megan James, and Paula Gluck.

I thank my husband, Jim McKinnell, for all his love, understanding, and continuing support, as well as my stepchildren and their spouses for their love and patience. One of the greatest gifts is to be blessed with two precious granddaughters.

It is said that creativity is a gift—something we inherit from those who have come before us. Therefore, I thank my parents and grandparents for this wonderful inheritance they passed on to me.

Available at all major bookstores.
Also available in ebook format.
www.BARNICLEandHUSK.com

SDP Publishing Solutions

SDPPublishing.com
Contact us at: info@SDPPublishing.com